Christmas Mice!

Christmas Mice!

by Bethany Roberts

illustrated by Doug Cushman

Clarion Books • New York

Clarion Books
a Houghton Mifflin Company imprint
215 Park Avenue South, New York, NY 10003
Text copyright © 2000 by Barbara Beverage
Illustrations copyright © 2000 by Doug Cushman

The illustrations for this book were executed in watercolor.
The text was set in 24-point Stone Serif.

Printed in the USA

Library of Congress Cataloging-in-Publication Data
Roberts, Bethany
Christmas mice! / by Bethany Roberts ; illustrated by Doug Cushman.
p.   cm.
Summary: A group of mice have fun as they go about their preparations for Christmas.
ISBN 0-395-91204-0
[1. Mice—Fiction. 2. Christmas—Fiction. 3. Stories in rhyme.]
I. Cushman, Doug, ill. II. Title.
PZ8.3.R5295Ch   2000
[E]—dc21   98-51133
CIP
AC

WOZ   10   9   8   7   6   5   4   3   2   1

To Melissa—Merry Christmas
—B.R.

To Valerie and Monica and the gang at Hicklebees
—D.C.

Christmas mice
deck the house.

Wreath the door.
Pound, pound, pound!

Christmas mice
wrap lots of presents.

Shiny ribbons,
round and round!

Christmas mice
trim the tree.

Put a star
on the top, top, top!

11

Christmas mice
bake yummy goodies.

Flour everywhere.
Mop, mop, mop!

Christmas secrets.
Stop! Don't peek!

Now out in the snow
to sing, sing, sing!

Merry, merry!
Joy, joy, joy!

Jingle bells!
Ring, ring, ring!

Across the sky—
a spot, a streak.

"Peace to all!"
Did you hear that?

Look—a paw print
in the snow.

Someone's been here!
Yikes! The cat!

What's this? A gift!
"From Cat to Mice."

A Christmas cheese!
Oh, yum, yum, yum!

The cat has caught
our Christmas cheer!

Now let's thank
our new-found chum.

Wrap one last gift—
"From Mice to Cat."

Tie it with
a big red bow.

Leave it here,
right by her door.

"Merry Christmas—

"Ho, ho, ho!"